MW00978328

Desdemona's Dreams

VOLUME 3

A Song of Dreams

Written by Z. W. Mohr

Illustrated by Aaron Damon Porter

Desdemona's Dreams LLC - New Orleans

COPYRIGHT ©2018
BY Z.W. MOHR AND AARON DAMON PORTER.
ALL RIGHTS RESERVED. NO PART OF THIS PUBLICATION MAY BE
REPRODUCED, DISTRIBUTED, OR TRANSMITTED IN ANY FORM OR BY
ANY MEANS, INCLUDING PHOTOCOPYING, RECORDING, OR OTHER
ELECTRONIC OR MECHANICAL METHODS, WITHOUT THE PRIOR
WRITTEN PERMISSION OF THE PUBLISHER, EXCEPT IN THE CASE OF
BRIEF QUOTATIONS EMBODIED IN CRITICAL REVIEWS AND CERTAIN
OTHER NONCOMMERCIAL USES PERMITTED BY COPYRIGHT LAW.
FOR PERMISSION REQUESTS, WRITE TO THE PUBLISHER,
ADDRESSED "ATTENTION: PERMISSIONS COORDINATOR,"
AT THE ADDRESS BELOW.

MOHR, Z.W. AND PORTER, AARON DAMON
DESDEMONA'S DREAMS VOLUME 3: A SONG OF DREAMS
WRITTEN BY Z.W. MOHR
AND ILLUSTRATED BY AARON DAMON PORTER
ISBN 978-0-9968874-4-1

DESIGN AND LAYOUT: DARE PORTER, REAL TIME DESIGN
ART PHOTOGRAPHY: MADELEINE WIEAND
Z.W. MOHR PHOTO BY SHADOW ANGELINA
AARON DAMON PORTER PHOTO BY KAULT PHOTOGRAPHY

10 9 8 7 6 5 4 3 2 1

DESDEMONA'S DREAMS LLC
4229 N DERBIGNY STREET
NEW ORLEANS, LOUISIANA 70117

E-MAIL: INFO@DESDEMONASDREAMS.COM

FOR JIM AND PETER

MAY WE NEVER BE DIVIDED AGAIN

~ Z.W. MOHR ~

Prologue

When we last left our heroine, there was an adventure afoot. With the faerie Puck, Desdemona flew through the air on a magic carpet marveling at the wonders of Mar's sky all around them. Fluffy multi-colored clouds formed unicorns prancing and giants dancing, while the land of Mar's sun, being a temperamental creature, shone its rays in only the directions it desired. Thankfully, it had grown fond of watching Desdemona and Puck, or else their search for the evil Pirate Moren would have gone quite dark. It's here, with the merry laughs of Puck and Desdemona flying through the air, that our tale begins anew, as they head towards the Swamp of Dreary Doings, with Desdemona unaware of the gravity of her quest, and the grave trials she must soon go through.

Desdemona holds on tightly as an icy wind blows, Puck laughing merrily as the carpet twists and turns to and fro. They pass over forests filled with trees singing in harmonies so infectious that our adventurers hum the wild tunes of leaves and needles. Twisting around mountains, soaring next to griffins and giant eagles, they even keep pace with a strange gathering of blue dogs made of balloons chasing a flock of purple seagulls. Their magic carpet slows as they make their way towards a swamp of

bubbling mud. As they lower, the popping mud bubbles release an overwhelming stench. Every time one pops, the air fills with the smell of rotten eggs, making Desdemona and Puck hold their collective breath.

Right before the flying carpet lands upon a patch of somewhat dry ground, Desdemona clasps onto its fabric, and draws in one big breath to avoid the closest popping bubble's stench. With her breath held she wakes up back in her bedroom, surrounded by rays of a less temperamental sun welcoming her to the new day.

The Stink of Adventure

"Blegh!" Desdemona spits out her held breath as she sits upright in her bed.

Teddy lets out a rumbly laugh from his spot next to her on the bed, "You must be near the Swamp of Dreary Doings if you're needing to hold your breath. If memory serves, that's one of the stinkiest places in Mar."

"It smelled like rotten eggs, Teddy. When I woke up I was afraid I would still smell like that place," Desdemona sniffs at her clothing to make sure she didn't bring the smell of swamp mud bubbles out with her.

"Thankfully, smells haven't learned to leave the world of dreams with you," Teddy chuckles a bit more.

Desdemona scowls at her bear, "Are you saying that, if I fall into any of that stinky mud, I might come out smelling like rotten eggs?"

Teddy tries to look seriously at Desdemona, but a smile still sneaks through, "I wouldn't test that theory, my lady. It could prove to be a dream that might not wash away so easily upon waking."

"Got it. No falling in the mud of the Swamp of Dreary Doings," Desdemona says as she gets up from her bed and realizes that she fell asleep in her dress.

"Perhaps a bath for you and a change of clothes, then we can partake in something fun. The day outside is beautiful and beckoning us to spend some time in the sun. We can have a picnic in the park!" Teddy proceeds to dance a few steps that Rina had taught them the night before.

"Hahaha," Desdemona laughs, "You're in cheery spirits this morning. You know I haven't solved the problem of the Pirate Moren, or the missing royal band. How can I think about going to the park with that left undone?" Desdemona replies as she heads over to her dresser to find something to wear.

"My lady, though that is a task of great importance, your well-being and joy are equally so. A happy heart can often lighten the heaviest of loads. As for my spirits, well...I never knew how much fun dancing was until Rina taught me. She is a truly spectacular dream." Teddy spins in a circle before laughing a grumbly laugh and bowing low.

"See, I told you dancing would be fun. By the way, where did my dream of dancing, ahem, I mean Rina, go?"

"After you went to sleep, I introduced her to the dolls in your dollhouse, and they all got along famously. They spent most of the night laughing at Cowboy Mouse's jokes, and didn't get to bed until quite late. I'm sure all of them are still sleeping soundly."

"Then I will leave them to their rest. Teddy, what should I wear for our picnic in the park? I'm thinking I'll put on my starry blue jeans, green unicorn shirt, and, of course, my red boots. I still feel like something is missing." Desdemona makes a pouty face at her clothing.

"Though I've no need of clothes, since I'm covered in such regal fur, I have heard it said that dressing the part helps to understand it. Perhaps your scarlet scarf tied around your head like a pirate. We can go have a wonderful picnic under the trees. You may even find some inspiration for the answers to the problems of Mar." Teddy pats Desdemona's leg.

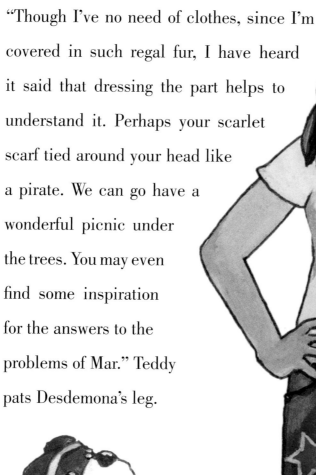

Desdemona finds her scarlet scarf and ties it around her head. "Yarrr!" she yells, crooking a finger as if it were a hook, "You're right, Teddy. I do feel more like a pirate with this scarf."

"Don't forget to take a bath. Though you may not have fallen in the Swamp of Dreary Doings, you could use a bit of scrubbing. When you're done, come and get me and we'll sail downstairs to see what delicious plunder we can take with us to the park!" Teddy replies with his best pirate impersonation.

Desdemona grabs a blue scarf from her dresser and ties it around Teddy's head, "Now you'll look piratey as well," she laughs while ruffling Teddy's head before heading out of the room.

Freshly bathed, dressed, and ready for adventure, Desdemona and Teddy make their way down the stairs, doing their best pirate impressions for each other. Before reaching the bottom, Desdemona trips and begins to topple forward. Luckily her Aunt Lulu Ann appears and catches her up in a giant hug.

"You really must watch where you're stepping, little niece. You never know when the world around you might get all topsy-turvy. Best to watch your feet so they don't come out from under you, or get unduly stuck." Aunt Lulu Ann squeezes Desdemona one more time, laughs, and then sets her down.

"I know these stairs like the back of my hand," Desdemona declares, as she looks back to see a picnic basket sitting on the third step up. "Where did that come from?"

"I filled a picnic basket for you, silly girl. Today is such a beautiful day, I thought to myself how lovely it would be for you two to go and listen to the songs of the wind in the trees."

"Teddy and I were talking about doing just that. Uhm...having a picnic that is." Desdemona imagines wind singing in the tree branches and smiles.

"Well, it's not the actual wind you should listen to, but the trees. They are such old and wondrous creatures, and they do sing songs if you take the time to listen." Lulu Ann's eyes were glimmering with gold flecks as she spoke of the trees.

"Desdemona," Teddy chimes in, "do you remember your favorite tree in the park?"

"Of course, Teddy. You told me her name is Xiara, and that she always loves when I spend time up in her branches. I just figured you told me that to make me happy," Desdemona replies.

"No, her name is really Xiara, and trees don't really talk, they just sing in sounds and pictures. If you close your eyes, you can see what they are singing. It's how many older creatures communicate with each other." Teddy smiles as he says this.

"How come you've never told me this before, Teddy?" Desdemona asks.

"Because it wasn't something you needed to know until now, oh curious kitten." Her Aunt Lulu Ann replies before Teddy can. "Besides, the day isn't getting any younger, so you best make your way to the park. Though, come to think of it, I don't know if it can get any older either," Lulu Ann chortles.

Teddy grumbles, "Ahem…my lady, we best get going. I'll climb into the basket until we get to a secluded spot at the park, and then I'll help you set up." Teddy opens one side of the wicker picnic basket and hops inside.

"Toodaloo!" Aunt Lulu Ann shouts as she opens the door and ushers Desdemona out of the house.

Before Desdemona can say anything else, the front door shuts and she's left on the stoop with the picnic basket on her right arm, "I know Aunt Lulu Ann is much cheerier than Aunt Lulu Bell, but sometimes her cheeriness seems more like hysteria, Teddy."

"Her whimsical nature borders on madness, my lady. Best to not think too much about it and just accept her for who she is." Teddy grumbles from inside the basket.

"I feel like I hardly know who my aunts are," Desdemona mutters, then she looks down the block towards Grayson Drab Elementary and starts to skip with the basket on her arm. She picks up speed as she passes her school, and hears Teddy's voice yelling, "Woah...too fast....GRRR! I have jam all over my fur," which makes her giggle all the way to the end of the block and up the hill towards the park.

Rocket and Roll

Desdemona skips to the engraved stone archway at the entrance of the park. A giant stone lion sits on the left with a smile upon his face and a ball balanced on one upraised claw, while on the right side is a statue of a fox, with reading glasses on its face and its nose buried in a stone book with the words "*The Wind in the Willows*" written upon its front. The archway above reads "*We are all just animals at play*" in giant letters that are impossible to ignore. Past the archway lie winding paths, groves of maple and oak trees, swings, slides, and all sorts of climbable things, with some children running and playing, and others looking more serious than children should ever look in a park.

"We're almost to Xiara, Teddy. Just the last stretch down the path towards the farthest trees, and then you can help me set up the picnic," Desdemona whispers to the picnic basket.

"Please, just take your time," grumbles Teddy, "I already have enough raspberry jam on my fur and would like to save the rest in the jar for scones your aunt packed."

Desdemona laughs at the thought of Teddy covered in jam, and then continues skipping, a little more attentive to how much she swings the picnic basket. Following the winding path that

leads past a group of grim-faced children, Desdemona makes it to her favorite tree. She looks around to make sure no other children or adults are watching, then knocks on the basket to tell Teddy it's safe to come out.

"Why don't you go ahead and swing on the swings while I set up the picnic, my lady." Teddy says as he pulls a napkin out of the basket to wipe jam from behind his ear.

"That's a great idea, Teddy!" Desdemona laughs and then runs off towards the swing set, "Maybe I'll swing high enough to kick a cloud."

"Just don't hurt yourself!" comes Teddy's reply, unheard by Desdemona because she was already running with excitement towards The Launch Pad, the name given to the swing-set by the more daring children.

Swinging, the air rushes around her, pressing against her

stomach as she WOOSHES forward, making her laugh harder and harder the higher she gets. Right when Desdemona gets as high as she thinks she can go without spinning entirely around the swing, she hears a loud, "WAHOOOOO!"

"We're almost touching the sun," comes the happy voice of a girl with rainbow-colored pigtails swinging next to Desdemona. "Are you going to launch?!" She asks, swinging right in time with Desdemona.

"I don't know, maybe...." Desdemona replies, still a bit startled that another girl is swinging next to her, and talking to her.

"Come on. On the count of three we can both launch. Let's be rocket ships together!" The pigtailed girl squeaks, "One!"

"I don't know if I'm ready to launch," Desdemona blurts out.

"Rockets don't need to get ready, only people do. Be a rocket ship. TWO!" shouts the excited girl.

"But how do we land?" Desdemona asks nervously.

"We don't worry about the landing, just the flying. THREE!"

Then they both let go and soar through the air towards the grass. Desdemona had only ever flown in her dreams before, and it feels amazing to fly through the park air, until she realizes that the ground is coming to meet her a bit faster than she wants.

"Now roll!" yells her pigtailed companion tumbling through the air next to her.

They hit the grass and roll for many feet before coming to a stop. Desdemona sits up from her final somersault and spits grass out of her mouth.

"Pbbbttt...Pbbbttt...Pbbbttt..."
Gross, Desdemona thinks. Knowing now for sure that though she loves the park, she has no desire to eat the park.

"Hahahahahahaha!" laughs the rainbow-pigtailed girl rolling around on the ground, "That was so much fun! I never get to play rockets with anyone anymore." Sitting up she smiles a big grin, showing the recent loss of one of her front teeth.

In spite of spitting out a bunch of grass, Desdemona can't stop smiling at the other girl. This was the first time in a long time that another child has actually wanted to play with her, and it makes everything about the day seem even better.

"My name is Casey C. My first name is spelled with a C, and my last name is too. My mother tells me I'm the untamed ocean between two C's. Or at least she used to." Says Casey, her blue eyes sparkling as she sits up and extends a hand.

"I'm Desdemona…" she responds, suddenly feeling a bit shy, since she isn't used to other kids talking to her. "I never knew my mother," she trails off, now feeling even more awkward as she shakes Casey's hand.

"That's okay. Mine drives me crazy sometimes. I think I've seen you at school, but you're a sixth grader so we haven't played together before. I'm only 8, but I'm big for my age." Casey stands up to prove how tall she is, her rainbow pigtails bobbing up and down on either side. Grass falls off of Casey's red t-shirt and green overalls, revealing the face of a lighter green frog with its red tongue grabbing a fly and the phrase "I LOVE TO FLY!" on the front.

"Your mom let you have rainbow-colored hair?" Desdemona asks, not really sure what to talk about.

"She doesn't really seem to care much about what I do anymore. When I told her I wanted rainbows for hair, she just said, 'Sure, whatever,' and let me put different color hair dyes into our shopping cart. I had to let my big sister do it though, because the directions didn't make a lot of sense to me. Since I promised to do her chores for the week, she didn't mind." Casey C. twirls her pigtails with her fingers.

"Thank you for playing rockets with me," Desdemona smiles. "I'd better get back to Teddy and our picnic."

"Who's Teddy?" Casey asks.

Desdemona didn't want to answer Casey at first, fearing that she'd be made fun of like the last time she'd told other kids about Teddy. Her aunts always told her she shouldn't tell other people about Teddy or their home, but it just didn't feel right lying to Casey.

"Teddy is my guardian teddy bear. He's setting up our picnic right now so that we can eat before the trees tell us stories," Desdemona replies, hoping Casey doesn't say something mean to her.

"That's AWESOME!" Casey dances around Desdemona repeating the word awesome at varying volumes. "I wish I had a teddy bear that could do all of those things. Mine looks good in the tutu I put him in, but he just sits there on my bed most of the time."

Desdemona briefly imagines Teddy in a tutu and giggles, "You believe me?"

"Why wouldn't I?" Casey quirks her head at Desdemona. "We were just rocket ships together, and rocket ships never lie to each other. Plus, maybe I can come play with you and Teddy sometime. Ooo…ooo…ooo…maybe we can play together at school. A lot of the other kids don't really play much anymore, and I get bored just playing by myself."

"I'd really like that," Desdemona smiles. "I'm going to head over to my picnic, but let's play together at school on Monday."

"See you at school!" shouts Casey as she runs off.

Rockets Make Fast Friends

Desdemona walks back to where Teddy has set up a beautiful picnic on top of a big blue blanket. There are all kinds of tasty things laid out for them to eat. There are lavender scones with raspberry jam and clotted cream, a bowl of blueberries, a platter with pieces of ham and turkey surrounded by slices of apples and pineapple, and two steaming cups of hot chocolate topped with cinnamon and marsh-mallows.

"I wondered if you were going to make it back, or if I would be forced to eat all of this delicious food myself," smiles Teddy.

"Teddy, I just met another little girl named Casey C, who wasn't afraid to play with me. She was full of imagination, and didn't even make fun of me for telling her about you," Desdemona gleefully dances around the picnic before sitting down.

"I thought your aunts told you not to tell anyone else about me, my lady?" Teddy quirks a furry brow at her.

"I know, but…well, she was just so friendly, and she actually played with me Teddy. We were rockets together!"

"Hmmm… I see. Well, I'm not going to chastise you too much about this, because I'm glad you've found a friend. Just try not to tell any others about our household. It's as much for their safety, as it is for yours." Teddy sits down across from Desdemona on the blanket, who has already started on the dessert course.

"Whafft thu joo men fo ver fafety?" comes Desdemona's scone-filled question.

"I'll assume that you are asking how people knowing about me could be unsafe for them? If I'm interpreting your mouthful-of-food speak right that is." Teddy asks.

"Yeff," responds Desdemona, trying her best to swallow the food in her mouth without choking.

"Well, my lady, without divulging too much information, I will tell you that there are certain creatures out in the world of dreams that could learn about you from other people's dreams. Your aunts have taken great care to keep your existence a secret from most of the dream world, until now anyways."

"Why, Teddy? I want to know why they've been protecting me, and from whom, or what?"

"And on my honor as your sworn guardian, I swear that answers will be found. There are tasks you must accomplish before you're ready for such knowledge, but I have faith in you, and know that you can accomplish anything you set your mind to." Teddy walks over to Desdemona and puts a paw on her shoulder, "Now, why don't we finish eating this scrumptious picnic so that Xiara can tell you a story. What she tells you will help in defeating the pirate Moren the Black Hand, and will also prepare you for adventures that lay ahead."

After they finish their picnic, Desdemona helps Teddy put everything back into the basket, which somehow never seems to become too full no matter how many items are put inside of it. Right before they sit back down on the blanket, Teddy looks up at Desdemona.

"Why don't you sit against Xiara's trunk and close your eyes," he motions towards the tree behind them.

"How is this going to help Xiara in telling me a story, Teddy?" Desdemona asks.

"Physical contact is important for all creatures, my lady. Notice how the roots of a tree go deep into the ground, and how their branches reach outwards towards the clouds. This is how they are in constant contact with the stories of earth and sky. Everything that happens in-between those two things fall within the realm of their knowledge, even dreaming. Trees are custodians of so much knowledge that they sing of it on the wind, to share what they know with other creatures that know how to listen."

Leaning back against Xiara's trunk, "How do I listen, Teddy?"

"Close your eyes…nestle yourself into her trunk as if it were the softest pile of blankets warming in the rays of the sun," Teddy's voice rumbles lower. "Let all other sounds fall away from you, as if they were the dust of this earth tumbling from your body as you stand. Even my voice is as distant as thunder rolling far off behind the mountaintops, until the blades of grass growing towards the sky are the only sounds you can hear."

Desdemona begins to feel light, as if she were made of nothing but feathers and wind.

An image of a sunny beach begins to fill Desdemona's mind as she slips into Xiara's storytelling of things already happened, and knowledge of what must be done.

Two Halves Make a Whole

On this day there was a king,

Merrily walking by the sea with his band at his side,

Not wary of a thing.

Then dark clouds formed in front of the sun.

Thunder crashed, and lightning flashed,

As the rain began to fall upon everyone.

A skeletal winged horse landed in front of the king.

Atop the terrifying creature sat a pale rider with gleaming red eyes

And a midnight cloak that twitched as if it were actually living.

The rider drew his curved silver sword,

Pointed it at the king and said,

"No more order, only chaos must move forward!

"Your kingdom is far too balanced for my liking,

I want the dreams of your land to run amuck.

I want them to rampage through the dream world like pillaging Vikings."

The King of Mar fell to his knees, cowering before the pale rider.

"Sire, I have always done as you've commanded,

Since the beginning when you created Mar in all its splendor.

"I govern the lost dreams, and give them purpose until they are needed.

I make sure they are hail, hearty, and ready,

In case any of the Lords of Dreams has tasks that need to be completed."

"Are you questioning me, oh King?!

That pathetic creature you once knew

Is now nothing!

"I am your new master, and I wish for chaos to reign.

I want the mind of every dreaming creature

To feel a new kind of loss and pain.

"I see rebellion in your sniveling glance,

And will brook no argument over what I want done.

Hmmm…how should I take away that chance?"

The king and his band shivered with fear

At the terrifying figure before them,

Wishing they could be anywhere but here.

"HAHAHA! I have the perfect plan.

Since you seem too harmonious in your existence,

I will turn you into a divided man.

"To start this world on its way to being chaotic and free

I shall split its ruler down the middle,

So that forever the king and his kingdom divided shall be.

"One half of you only wanting happiness and fun,

While the other half is striving

To make this world come undone.

"I shall twist the song of dreaming with which I bound this land,"

Pointing at the musicians,

"And the only ones able to play its counter will be your royal band.

"Your royal band shall reside with your darker half,

Being the only ones able to piece you back together,

And you'll feel only pain and confusion, when you should ever feel wrath.

"Salvation will forever be right outside your reach,

Leaving you drowning in a shallow sea of happiness,

Which you will never breach."

The pale rider sang a song, a piercing melody,

Binding each note to his blade

With razor-sharp duplicity.

Drawing closer he swung his sword.

From where the King stood there now were two,

A complacent King staring blankly as a fierce pirate stepped forward.

Where the King wore a smile, this pirate wore a scowl.

His pirate beard was long and black with skulls braided in,

And his nose is curved like the beak of an owl.

A blue sash was tied around his blood-red coat,

That extended all the way down to his shiny black boots,

And instead of a left hand he had the curved black horn of a goat.

With eyes of a raging storm,

The pirate creature in front of the king

Smiled wickedly as it took in its own terrifying form.

The pale figure laughed menacingly,

As lightning crashed across the sky,

And he waved a clawed hand at the sea.

"You shall be Moren the Black Hand,

Dread pirate of these dream seas,

And scourge of all the land.

"This royal band shall keep you company,
The song of binding hidden inside them,
With no one here to set it free.

"They will play pirate dirges upon your ship
As you make your way across Mar's seas
On delightfully destructive trips

"And you, little king, shall go back to your throne.
A smile will always plague your face,
But you will feel so very alone."

A pirate ship with skulls for sails appeared

And a motley-looking crew peered over its rails to yell,

"YARRRRR! Captain, we be here!"

The pale figure waved his sword once more,

And Moren the Black Hand and the royal band

Were transported to the ship from the shore.

The rider rears back on his skeletal steed,

As the nightmare issued a terrible scream from its lips,

And the rider cackles once more at his terrible deed.

A resounding chorus of cannon fire exploded from the ship's guns,

And both horse and rider leapt into the sky

To fly off into the storm cloud covered sun.

The King started whistling to himself some merry old tune,

Continuing to walk down the beach,

Seemingly unaware of the trouble coming soon.

Then Desdemona finds herself sitting on the sand,

The King of Mar has since faded away,

As has the pirate ship and royal band.

Remnants are all that is left of the King's whistled tune,

Floating on the sea breeze,

And dancing between each individual sand dune.

Desdemona listens closely to the melody;

The notes reminding her of swaying sunflowers

Bound to the earth, but also free.

A hint of light,

A touch of cinnamon,

A whisp of night,

A laughing owl,

A soft whisper,

A loud howl,

A tender tear,

A wayward fear,

The love of something far, but near.

A balance of things so light and so deep,

A song of brightest wake,

And soundest sleep.

Hidden Meanings

The melody of the King of Mar's tune still circling around in her thoughts, Desdemona opens her eyes with the music tumbling from her lips. Looking up from her dream against the tree, Desdemona spots Teddy sitting by the picnic basket, and gazing at her rather inquisitively.

"How was your story, my lady?" Teddy asks.

"It was terrifying, Teddy. There's some evil creature trying to destroy the Land of Lost Dreams. He flew out of the sky upon a nightmare of a horse and somehow divided the King of Mar into two separate beings. No wonder the King seems so confused and crazy, he's only half the person he used to be. At least his odd behavior makes so much more sense."

"That is most disturbing indeed, my lady. But, perhaps a topic best discussed back in the safe confines of our home," Teddy reaches out a furry paw and pats Desdemona's leg.

"Ok, Teddy. Let's pack everything up so we can go home. I need to talk to you about what I saw," Desdemona gets up and starts to head towards the park's entrance, "and maybe I should talk to my aunts about this as well," she adds in an unsure tone.

The trip back to her house is accompanied by a more somber

tone, that Teddy comments on when he realizes Desdemona's just shuffling her feet, and not skipping.

"I'm sure Xiara's tale seems quite dire, but mirth and whimsy are some of the surest agents to defeat the foulest beings. When faced with weighty decisions, my lady, one should not let them hold you down with their gravity," Teddy says as they arrive at the iron rose gate in front of their home.

Desdemona looks up and notices that the gargoyle isn't on top of their house anymore.

"Teddy, where did our house gargoyle go?" Desdemona asks with a touch of worry in her voice.

Teddy pushes the lid of the picnic basket open enough to see the front of the house, "Hmmm…that makes for a strange turn of events. They usually send him out only when it's darkest night."

Desdemona pushes open the gate and heads up the amethyst stone pathway, "It can't be stranger than most of my life in this house, and will most likely be explained away with nonsense once I ask," Desdemona states aloud as she makes her way up the stairs and opens the front door.

Right as Desdemona passes the threshold of their house, her Aunt Lulu Ann jumps out of the library with a vibrant gold and

black pirate hat upon her head, very bright pirate attire, and swinging a cutlass in the most whimsical of manner.

"Avast, me niece! Hast thou heard the trees, and whispered secrets pon' the wind?! Will ye be able to save the Land of Lost Dreams, from its tumult that resides within? Hahahahaha!" Aunt Lulu Ann bursts out laughing as she sticks the cutlass in her left hand into their wooden floor to wobble back and forth.

Desdemona shakes her head at Aunt Lulu Ann's pirate performance, but can't keep from smiling. "I'm not completely sure how to solve the problems of Mar, which you seem to know about as well. I would ask you how you know, but I feel like that would lead to some silly game that I don't want to play."

"It might do just that, little niece," comes the smirking reply from Aunt Lulu Ann, "but, I would still ask you what you learned from Xiara."

"I learned what happened to the King of Mar, and beyond that….all I can do is whistle you a tune I heard lingering on the lost sea breeze," Desdemona states in an exasperated tone.

"A tune you say? A tune in a dream? One would think that music, coming from the Land of Mar, would hold some sort of sway upon important things. Perhaps you shouldn't discount the entirety of your day, but instead learn from each piece accordingly?" Aunt Lulu Ann smiles her annoyingly knowing smile.

"Perhaps I will," Desdemona retorts, not entirely sure to what she just tentatively agreed.

"There is no PERHAPS, only that you will," comes a dry crackling voice from their library.

The look of fear that fills Desdemona's face is so tangible that Teddy can feel it from within the picnic basket. He hops out of the picnic basket and pulls Desdemona close to whisper in her ear.

"It's alright, my lady. Your Aunt Lulu Bell may have a gruff exterior," he pauses, trying to find more pleasing words to describe Aunt Lulu Bell, but then continues anyways, "which still wouldn't hold a candle to the frightening interior, but she does have your best interests at heart, and is quite adept in the darker side of things. To take something and split its nature in two with malicious intention is only something that nightmares steeped in chaos do. It would be good for you to include Aunt Lulu Bell in this specific quest. She most assuredly will be able to help with the missing pieces to such a dastardly puzzle."

Nightmarish Reflections

Desdemona makes her way into their library, moving with all the speed of one knowing the destination is somewhere they'd rather not be. Maybe Teddy's right. Even though her Aunt Lulu Bell is often in a foul mood, she does tend to be easier to understand, even if the answers do seem a bit mean.

"Uh…I…uhm," Desdemona stutters as she enters the library, where Aunt Lulu Bell is staring out the window towards Remsy.

"Come closer! Speak up, girl! 'Uhm' is not a question that will suffice. You have important tasks to accomplish, and I expect you to articulate more clearly than that." Aunt Lulu Bell places her hand on her hip as she turns to glare at Desdemona.

Desdemona snaps out of her stupor and walks up to Aunt Lulu Bell, "I need to ask you about a tune I heard in a dream. It was playing on the wind right after some evil creature split the King of Mar into two separate beings. Aunt Lulu Ann and Teddy seem to think you would know what it is, or maybe, what it means?"

"Can you at least hum this tune for me? Or do I need to guess what it sounded like as well?" Aunt Lulu Bell's boney finger taps impatiently against her hip as she continues to scowl.

Desdemona begins to hum the tune for Lulu Bell, trying to remember as much of it as she can.

"Hmmm...Yes, that's The Song of Mar. It's the dream song that helped create the Land of Lost Dreams. Fitting...so clever of him, twisting the song that created the land into one that plunged it into chaos. I know it because I was there when it was first sung. Like most of creation, there is a song hidden inside of things. Now, tell me the rest of the story and don't dawdle. If I'm to help you, then we must move quickly before he catches on."

"Before who catches on? What was that terrifying creature that came out of the sky? And why does he want to destroy the Land of Mar?" Desdemona asks, trying to be less intimidated by her aunt Lulu Bell.

"Impudence will get you nowhere with me, niece," Aunt Lulu Bell pokes Desdemona's shoulder with a crooked fingernail, "But I do enjoy a show of bravery in the face of danger. And I know you find my face quite dangerous to look at." Lulu Bell gives a crooked toothed grin to Desdemona as she lets out a throaty chuckle.

"All right, I'll tell you this much for now and no more. That creature is who we've been grooming you to fight. It wants to destroy all dreams everywhere and turn the world into a place with no imagination, with no heart. If it gets its way, existence will become a grey and withered thing in which no new thoughts shall thrive, and eventually, all of humanity will just fade away. This is too much even for a being such as I." Lulu Bell turns her face away from Desdemona at this last statement.

"I didn't know I was being taught to fight something." Desdemona looks a bit confused, "What do you mean by, 'for something such as you?'"

"Not fighting in the normal sense, but sharpening your wits and mind, girl. Stop wasting time. I've given you your one answer, and you should consider that very generous. Now, tell me the rest of the story, and leave out not one single detail!" Lulu Bell exclaims in a tone that brooks no argument.

Desdemona knows she won't get anymore from her aunt, so she relates the rest of Xiara's story.

Upon Desdemona's completion of her story, Aunt Lulu Bell leans forward. "The song you heard, you know it deep inside of you. Much like Lulu Ann and me, you are connected to the dreaming, and feel its pulse as part of you. Use the band to break this curse, and bind what is two into one. Share the song that built their land, and this task will be done."

"What if that creature comes back to stop me?"

"He won't. There will be matters occupying his attention until you are done. But don't dawdle, and keep your eyes open for well-laid traps. Just because that creature isn't there doesn't mean others in his employ aren't."

Sticky Situations

Desdemona leaves the library in a daze. Things were changing so fast. Her life has always had magical happenings, things Desdemona was pretty certain other kids didn't have, but none of them had been so terrifying up until now.

"My lady?" comes the comforting grumble of Teddy's voice. "Are you ok?" He places a furry paw against Desdemona's knee as she is about to head upstairs.

"Did she tell you what you need to do to help the King of Mar?" Teddy asks.

"Yes… It was strange, but somehow made sense to me. I need to get back to The Swamp of Dreary Doings. That's where I'll find the pirate, and where I'll also find the royal band."

Desdemona starts walking towards her room with Teddy on her heels. "My lady, before you go back to the Land of Mar, I want to tell you something."

"What is it, Teddy?" Desdemona replies as they enter her room and she notices how dark it's become outside.

"I want you to know that you can pull yourself out of Mar if you need to. You can force yourself awake."

Desdemona looks down at her friend, "You mean I can just end my dream whenever I want to?"

"Yes. It's part of who you are. You have much more control in dreams than other people. The Land of Mar is an in-between space in the realms of dreams, so it's a place that's easier for you to go to and come from."

"But I thought they could've kept me as a prisoner there in the King's dungeon? How is that possible if I can just wake myself up?" Desdemona asks, more than a bit confused.

Teddy looks at Desdemona with a very serious expression on his bear face. "Well, you would've been bound by the laws of Mar if you had been taken prisoner by its ruler. That's why I pulled you out. Once you were recognized as a lost dream, which are the only dreams in Mar, you would've been considered a subject of its king. Just remember, as long as you aren't prisoner of a realm's ruler, you can come and go as you choose. Such are the laws of dreams for one such as you. There are a few exceptions to this, but none that you need to know right now."

Desdemona takes off her boots and lies down on her bed, "I want to help the King of Mar. I made a promise to find his royal band, and that pirate Moren needs to be stopped from destroying any more innocent dreams."

Teddy hops up on the bed and snuggles the purple pillow behind her head, "It's good to hear you feel confident about Mar, but please be careful, and remember to keep an eye on Puck. He may not have your best interests at heart."

"I will. I promise. Tell Rina she'll have more company soon. I plan on having guests with me from Mar."

And then Desdemona closes her eyes and lets herself drift off into that floating haze. Feeling the world fall away, the putrid stench of mud bubbles surrounds her once again.

X Marks The Spot

Desdemona's eyes open as the flying carpet hovers above the mud.

She watches Puck touch the ground first,

Making sure he's not stuck in the bubbling crud.

Puck stands there and laughs,

Turns his head towards Desdemona and winks,

"It's solid enough, you won't need a raft."

Desdemona steps off the carpet and breathes in the foul air.

"Who would want to live in this disgusting place

That smells like wet dog hair."

About twenty paces in front of them lies a house made of mud,

With dirt-smudged windows

And a roof that looks like dried cud.

Out of the house rambles an eight-foot-tall mud creature.

He oozes more than walks

And mud that falls off him is his most attractive feature.

"Who trespasses in my swamp?"

He burbles from his mud mouth

"Whoever ya are, I'll give ya a womp!"

"Ho there, and hey there, my slurpish Sludge fellow!"

Puck chortles and prances as he reaches into a pouch at his hip,

And pulls out a flower that shines as if it were made of the sun's fiery yellow.

"I sent you a secret on the wind

Telling of the girl

Who wants to bring about Moren's end.

"And this flower, my friend, is a gift from me to you.

To make sure that you're willing to help

With what I asked you to do."

"Why would Sludge want a boring flower?"

Sludge replies, never taking his eyes off of it,

As if it held him in its power.

"Hmmm…perhaps I was wrong about this one?"

Puck grins, making to put it back in his pouch.

"It's made of firebird dreams, with nectar from a burning sun.

"Most rare, I assure you, but I have my ways.

It can be found every hundred years or so

Growing beneath the spot where a phoenix lays its egg."

"I'll make that promise if you follow my terms, oh tricky friend.

I want you to make yourself look like me and summon Moren,

Convince him to have his band play you a song before he gives you your end.

You'll have to wait until I return, so don't wiggle too much.

The mud seems to be sinking very slowly,

But I can't help you if you're too far under for me to touch."

At this Puck looks surprised and aghast.

"But, where are you going?

If you're gone too long I won't last."

"That's none of your concern.

Just be ready to fulfill your part of our bargain

As soon as I return."

With that Desdemona runs back towards the flying carpet.

She whispers, "Take me to the King as fast as you can."

Then holds on tight, determined not to fall off of it.

Flying back to the palace and into the throne room,

Desdemona runs past all the waiting creatures,

Avoiding their looks of irate gloom.

"King! Oh great King! I've found you something truly amazing.

It's a flower growing in The Swamp of Dreary Doings that sings your praises.

You must come with me to see this incredible thing."

Before any of the court can object,

Desdemona grabs the King's hand

And pulls him onto the carpet.

Desdemona begs the carpet to fly as fast as it can.

They zip through the air back towards the grass X,

Now showing only Puck's shoulders, head, and flower filled hand.

Jumping off the carpet,

Desdemona takes the King by the hand,

"Avoid the mud puddles Your Majesty, or you'll get more than wet."

The King stops in place, "Why is Puck up to his neck in mud?

Is the flower in his hand the one that sings my praises?

Shouldn't we save it before it's covered in that disgusting crud?"

Desdemona points to the largest tree she can see,

"Just head over behind that tree, oh wondrous King.

You'll get more than just the praises of a flower if you listen to me."

"Harumph…I'm the King of Mar, young lady, and I don't like surprises!"

Desdemona looks around at her surroundings,

And a plan arises.

"You see, your majesty, the flower will only sing your praises if you're not staring.

It is a very shy flower, too bashful to compliment you to your face.

When I left, it was telling a tale of your deeds of great daring."

The King puffs up his chest,

"Well those must be true, even if I can't remember them.

I'll go behind the tree so I can hear it talk about how I'm the best!"

Desdemona calls to Puck, "Summon Moren!"

Puck lets out a long strange sounding whistle,

Echoing after he stops, as if it doesn't know how to end.

Off in the distance Desdemona can hear the chorus of the pirate crew,

Their swords banging and clanging,

Music being played to their trudging as they slog their way through.

Desdemona ducks behind the King's tree,

"One last thing, Puck,

Don't forget to make yourself look like me."

"How did you know I can change my shape?" Puck looks surprised.

"I didn't, until you just told me,

But figured if I just told you to, then you wouldn't get the chance to have lied."

"You are a clever girl," Puck says with a wicked grin,

And then he shimmers and changes to look like Desdemona,

At least the parts of him that showed from the mud he was trapped in.

Then Desdemona hears the voice of the dread Pirate Moren.

"So, yar be the trouble maker t'was searching for me?!

Now yar've found me, yar going to meet yar terrible end!"

There stands Moren the Black Hand,

With his black goat horn pointed at Puck,

And behind him stand his men and the royal band.

"I have one last request, oh pirate lord.

Let your infamous band play me a funeral dirge,

Before you drag me off to the Devil's horde."

Moren's eyes rage like lightning crashing,

Turning from greys to blues to violent purples,

The skulls in the braids of his beard still clanging and bashing.

"Tis fine wit me if thar be music heard on this day.

Always better to have some rhythms

When thar be a dream for me to flay."

"Yarrr!!!" cry Moren's men as the terrified looking band begins to play.

At that moment Desdemona pushes out the now trembling King,

And jumps out herself into the light of the swamps gloomy day.

Desdemona begins to whistle the tune from Xiara's story,

The notes of the song take physical form as they circle the musicians,

Filling them with the Song of Mar, which they begin to play in all its glory.

Desdemona's hair flies all around her as her feet lift off the ground.

The Pirate Moren tries to run, but finds he's pulled towards the King,

Both of them held captive by the dream song sound.

Desdemona's emerald eyes begin to glow, as words form without thought,

As if she'd known this song all along,

And had only just forgot.

"A hint of light,

A touch of cinnamon,

A whisp of night,

"A laughing owl,

A soft whisper,

A loud howl,

"A tender tear,

A wayward fear,

The love of something far, but near.

"A balance of brightest light and darkest deep,

A song of ever-waking,

And soundest sleep.

"A song of deepest mind.

A song to build.

A song to seek and find.

"It will begin and end;

Song of Mar bring two together,

That one did rend."

Notes of music swirl around Moren and the King

Pushing them closer together

Until a flash of light erupts, blinding everyone and thing.

Desdemona opens her eyes to the King standing in front of her,

But instead of his usual befuddled look, his eyes were shining and bright.

"My girl, you truly are a wonder!"

Right at that moment Puck lets out a shout.

"Don't forget about our deal.

How are you going to get me out?"

Desdemona smiles and replies, "Put the flower in the mud and dig yourself out."

Once done, the mud starts to harden and crack.

"You were so surprised, that you forgot about what happened to Sludge, you lout."

The King rests his hand on Desdemona's shoulder,

"Thank you, girl, for rescuing me from myself.

I don't know why the Dream Lord split me like lightning to a boulder.

Forever will you have my aide as long as you're in my lands.

What boon would you ask

From these newly returned King's hands?"

Desdemona looks towards the four musicians surrounded by piles of sand.

When that evil creature's spell was broken it must have unraveled Moren's crew,

And freed the now confused looking band.

Seeing a mandolin, accordion, flute, and drum between the musicians,

Desdemona thinks of how happy Rina will be with live music,

And comes quickly to her decision.

"I'd like to take your band with me,

For I have a dancer that needs more music to dance to.

Yes, that is the wish I want you to grant me."

The King smiles so brightly, and waves his hand at the band.

"They are yours for the taking, fair lady.

Know that you will always have my assistance whenever I can."

Desdemona walks towards the band and tells them to come in close.

She has them all join hands as she wishes herself awake,

Just as Teddy told her she could if too much danger arose.

The Song That Changed It All

Appearing back on her bed the four band members fall into Teddy's lap. Teddy tries to untangle himself from all of them, removing the mandolin dangling from his ear fur.

"That's quite an earring you have there." Desdemona giggles.

"Grrr….", Teddy grumbles as he gets it loose and hands it back to the worried looking musician, "I love music, but I don't need to wear it. How about you tell me about what happened in Mar, my lady."

Desdemona motions for all of them to sit in a circle near the dollhouse as Rina comes out of the house to join them, the band sees Rina and strike up a beautiful melody. She can't help but dance the rest of the way to their sitting circle. Desdemona and Teddy join in the dancing for a minute, then they all sit back down as Desdemona begins to tell them all the tale of her adventures in Mar. At the end of her harrowing adventure everyone claps, except Teddy.

"Aren't you impressed, Teddy? I outsmarted Puck, returned the King of Mar to his old self, and brought his royal band back here with me." Desdemona smiles at her bear.

"I am, my lady. I knew you could defeat the Pirate Moren, and I'm glad you outsmarted Puck. He's a dastardly tricky one, probably deserving worse treatment than you gave him." Teddy's expression remains very serious.

"Then why aren't you happy for me, Teddy?" Desdemona asks, feeling a bit confused.

"You sang a song of dream creation, my lady. Your powers have grown quite quickly. It means that things will soon get harder, and the challenges you face will be much fiercer. Your aunts know this, and soon the thing of shadows and despair shall know it too. I worry that I won't be able to protect you."

Desdemona comes over and wraps her arms around her bear.

"You'll always keep me safe, Teddy. I believe in you."

Something Wicked This Way Comes...

In the library of their house, aunts Lulu Ann and Lulu Bell shut the giant tomes they were both gazing into; one sister bright and shining, the other looking as if the light itself feared touching her.

"He's right you know," comes the dusty voice of Lulu Bell.

"Of course I know," Lulu Ann retorts haughtily, "it's only a matter of time before he comes for her."

"The way here will still be long and winding, but when she's in other dream realms there's not much we can do to hide her." Lulu Bell taps her right hand's long fingernails on the armrest off her blood red cushioned chair. "The best we can hope for is that he still underestimates how much of a threat she is."

"She did sing a dream song!" titters Lulu Ann as she claps her hands. "Maybe she'll be ready to face him sooner than we think."

"To be honest, I wasn't sure that was going to work. But I figured that if it failed she would learn how to fight off a hoard of pirates right quick, and that's a valuable lesson as well." Lulu Bell sits forward and smiles a wicked crooked smile.

"Morose to your core, sister. What would our brother say if he were here?" chides Lulu Ann.

"We may find that out much sooner than we wish…"

To be continued . . .

Z.W. Mohr was born in the foothills of Los Angeles, between a wild blaze and a mudslide. Being raised on stories told by firelight, and traveling to hidden temples of long gone civilizations at a young age, might have unlocked doors of imagination he's never learned how to close. Knowing that the best castles are built from dreams, he learned the masonry of language so he could build castles of his own. The stories of Desdemona are an invitation to visit these castles. Please pack lightly. Wear your heart on your sleeve so that the gatekeeper knows it's you, keep a secret in your pocket to trade for treasure, and leave this realm only when you have your own dream to go to.

Acknowledgements

Though writing itself can be a lonely business, with mainly your characters to keep you company while in the thick of it, there are so many people that helped in the creation of this finished book. Thanks to: my family – you believe in what I create, even when I question myself, and for that I'm eternally grateful; my partner Casey – for being the best muppet ever; Mike Lasage – for your friendship, and creativity, in recording my audiobooks; my editors – Geoff Munsterman, Zach Bartlett, Andy Reynolds, Carin Chapman, and Casey Coren, you're all invaluable; Dare Porter – your design and layout skills turn mine, and Aaron's, work into such beautiful finished products, thank you; Aaron Porter – without you this series wouldn't be the wonder it's become, you are a dear friend, and amazing artist; Archanna Byrd – You have a whole life of creating ahead, and I can't wait to see what else you come up with; and last, but not least, to all of the fans that send us mail, or post up videos and pictures online showing their love of *Desdemona's Dreams*, you mean the world to me. The world is what you make it!

Archanna Byrd lives with her family in New Orleans, is 15 years old, and a former Arise Academy student, now attending Morris Jeff Community School. She's a budding young writer, illustrator, and painter, with an interest in trying her hand at as many types of art as she can. Muffin is her first published character, and one day she hopes to be a full-time storyboard artist for movies. She'd like to thank her family and friends for all of their love and support, and can't wait to put more art out into the world.

Aaron Damon Porter, Aaron Damon Porter was born in Oakland, California, where he learned quickly that Mr. Sketch scented markers are not, in fact, edible.

Aaron attended arts-focused schools through middle and high school, then studied art with a focus in painting at the University of California at Santa Cruz, earning his bachelor's degree in 2008. Shortly thereafter, he moved to New Orleans, Louisiana and has been pursuing a living as a full-time working artist ever since. Aaron displays and sells his original work as a permitted artist in Jackson Square, and has thus far had his illustration work published in four books, three of which are the original series, *Desdemona's Dreams.*

Acknowledgements

With each step along the narrative path of *Desdemona's Dreams*, I feel my world expanding. The relationships and the creative work involved with the project are ever deepening, and I am grateful.

For this volume, I would like to thank again our Dream Team: Zach, Dare, and Maddy. Thanks also to Tony and Aria, studio mates extraordinaire, and to Brian and Humphrey on the home front. And last but not least, thank you to Lisa and Greg at Creason's Fine Arts Gallery for always having my back when it comes to art supplies, shop talk, and encouragement.